Big Black Horse

16/5/2/1935

38/195

BIG BLACK HORSE

Adapted from *The Black Stallion* by

WALTER FARLEY

Illustrated by JAMES SCHUCKER

Prepared under the supervision of JOSETTE FRANK,
Children's Book Adviser of the Child Study Assn. of America

THIS SPECIAL EDITION IS PUBLISHED BY ARRANGEMENT WITH
THE PUBLISHERS OF THE REGULAR EDITION
RANDOM HOUSE INC.
BY
E. M. HALE AND COMPANY
EAU CLAIRE, WISCONSIN

THE BIG BLACK HORSE

The story of a boy's love for a horse. By WALTER FARLEY
Illustrated by JAMES SCHUCKER.
Adapted from The Black Stallion.

A fierce black horse was loaded onto the ship that Alec Ramsey was coming home in from India. What a time they had getting him on board. Alec took sugar to the horse and tried to make friends. When the ship was wrecked Alec freed the horse and the horse pulled Alec to the island where the two became great friends. When Alec was rescued he insisted upon taking the horse. This is an exciting horse story illustrated with excellent pictures.

*

This book, especially designed for young children, is a brief retelling of the first part of a famous book entitled THE BLACK STALLION and originally published by Random House in 1941. When the children are a little older, they will want to read the whole story, many times longer than this, just as it was written by Walter Farley.

Published in New York by Random House, Inc. and
simultaneously in Toronto, Canada by Random House of Canada Limited

Library of Congress Catalog Card Number: 53-6288

Manufactured in the U.S.A.

In a country far across the sea lived a big black horse. He had a long tail, a long mane, and long legs. His head was small, and so were his ears, but his eyes were large and bright. He had always run wild and free. He had no name—he was just called the Black.

One day some men caught him, blindfolded him, and tried to put him on a ship. They pulled him hard with long ropes and hit him with whips. The Black became very angry. He rose high on his hind legs and pawed the air. Then he screamed and plunged forward, hitting one of the men with his hoofs. The man fell to the ground and lay still. For a long while the big black horse fought hard, but at last the men held him and managed to get him onto the ship. He was pulled into a small stall and tied. Then the door was firmly shut and bolted, and the ship steamed away.

On the deck of that ship red-haired Alec Ramsay was standing alone. His parents had sent him to visit his uncle in India, and now he was on his way home to the United States and back to school.

Alec had watched the fight between the men and the horse, and he felt very sorry for the big Black. The boy loved horses, and always got along well with them. Never in his life had he used a whip on a horse.

Day after day, as they sailed the sea, Alec listened to the Black trying to break out of his stall. He heard the strong hoofs crashing against its wooden sides. The Black was the wildest horse he had ever seen!

One night Alec went to the horse's stall, carrying in his hand some lumps of sugar. It was so dark inside the stall he couldn't see the horse. He could hear him, though! So Alec talked to the Black. He told him that he was his friend and that he would never harm him. After a long while Alec left the lumps of sugar on top of the stall door and went to his cabin. Later, when he returned, the sugar was gone.

Every night after that Alec would go to the Black's stall, leave the sugar, and go away. Sometimes he would see the Black, but at other times he would only hear the angry ring of hoofs against the floor.

One evening the air was hot and still. Heavy clouds blacked out the stars, and long streaks of lightning raced through the sky. When Alec went to the stall, the Black had his head over the door. He was looking out to sea, and his nostrils were sniffing the air. He turned, whistled when he saw Alec, then looked out to sea again.

Alec was very happy. It was the first time the Black hadn't drawn back into the stall at sight of him. He moved closer and put out some sugar. The Black looked at it, then at the boy. Slowly he moved nearer and began to eat the sugar. Alec watched him for a moment, knowing that the horse was beginning to trust him. Then he went back to his cabin.

He was awakened very suddenly in the middle of the night. A terrible storm had arisen, and Alec was thrown out of bed by the rolling of the ship. There were loud crashes of thunder, followed by flashes of lightning that made the cabin as bright as day.

With trembling hands, Alec hastily pulled on his clothes. Then he reached under his bunk for a life jacket, fastened it around him, and opened the door. Out in the passageway people were shouting and running. Suddenly there was a crash louder than any of the others. The ship shook. Alec heard someone shout, "She's been struck! We're sinking. The ship is going down!"

Alec ran up on deck and, looking about, saw people scrambling into lifeboats. As Alec waited his turn to get into a boat, he suddenly thought of the big black horse. What was happening to him? Was he still in his stall? He must be given a chance to be saved, too!

Fighting his way out of the crowd huddled at the rail,
Alec ran toward the stern of the ship.

He could hear the Black snorting and neighing. Alec
opened the stall door and the horse came rushing out,

for he had broken the rope that held him. The boy tried to get out of his way, but too late! As the big black horse plunged for an opening in the rail, he hit Alec's shoulder, knocking the boy into the sea with him. Alec felt the water close over his head.

Alec's life jacket brought him quickly to the surface again. As he turned to swim back to the ship, an explosion shook the air, and he saw that the ship was sinking rapidly. Frantically he looked around for a lifeboat, but there was none to be seen. Then suddenly he saw the Black, swimming close by. The broken rope still hung from the horse's halter. Without stopping to think, Alec grabbed hold of it. In another moment he was being pulled through the stormy sea!

All night long the Black swam, pulling Alec behind him. The boy was very, very tired and weak from battling the high waves, but the big horse kept on swimming steadily.

When morning came the storm had ended and the sea was quiet. Alec raised his head and looked about him. There, in the distance, was a white sandy beach!

Faster and faster swam the Black, and soon he was on the beach, pulling Alec right up on the sand.

Alec let go of the rope and lay still, exhausted. The big black horse had saved him from drowning!

Alec slept for a long while. When he awoke he felt much better, but he was very thirsty. In the sand he saw the hoof prints of the big horse. Alec got up and followed them, for he knew that the horse would find fresh water, if any was to be found.

He crossed the beach and climbed a hill. From where he stood, he could see all around. He was on a small island, mostly sandy and with only a few trees, bushes, and patches of grass showing.

Still following the Black's hoof prints, he went on until he came to a small pool of fresh water. And there was the Black beside it! The wild horse whistled and pawed furiously at the earth when he saw the boy, but made no move to harm him.

So Alec threw himself down on the ground, plunged his face into the cool, clear water, and drank and drank until he had had enough. Then he fell into a deep sleep again.

When he awoke the next morning he was terribly hungry. After all, he had gone a whole day and a half without eating. He must find some food. And he did. Not far from the spring was a berry bush, and he had to be satisfied with a meal of berries.

Now to make some sort of shelter for himself. He went to the beach, picked up some long pieces of driftwood, and dragged them back to the spring. With these he built a small shed.

All this work made him hungry again, but he was very tired and weak, too, so he lay down to rest. Nearby he saw the Black, moving from one place to another, looking for small patches of grass. "He's as hungry as I am," thought Alec as he closed his eyes.

The next morning Alec made his way toward the rocky side of the island. There he found a lot of sea moss growing on the rocks at the water's edge. He remembered reading that some kinds of sea moss could be eaten and would keep a person alive! He pulled off whole handfuls of the moss and hurried back to the spring with it. There he washed it carefully in the fresh water to take away the salty flavor of the sea, and set it out in the sun to dry.

25

After a little while Alec tasted it. It wasn't bad, and at least it would keep him from starving. He ate some more, and left the rest on the ground beside the pool. Would the Black eat it too? Alec hurried to his shelter and watched anxiously. Soon the horse rushed up, shook his head, and took a long drink of water. Next he put his nose to the ground and walked over toward the moss. He sniffed at it first, then tasted a little of it. Then he ate it all.

That night Alec slept better than at any time since he had been on the island. He had found food for his horse and for himself.

From that day on, the big black horse knew that Alec was his friend. He was still a very wild horse. But the boy was kind to him, so the Black never snorted or kicked or showed his teeth when Alec came near him. Instead, he came when he was called, and ate all the sea moss the boy brought him. At last something even more wonderful happened. One day the Black let Alec climb upon his back and ride him all around the island.

Never had Alec ridden such a wonderful horse! He was as swift as the wind. Every day after that Alec rode the Black up and down the beach. Sometimes the horse would rear when Alec tried to mount him, but the boy would speak softly in his ear, and then the Black would quiet down.

Alec grew to love the Black and to wonder how he could get him home. He wanted to keep him in a fine barn and take care of him. He wanted to ride him in the park and show him to his friends. But how would either of them ever get off this island?

They had been on it for nineteen days, and the weather was turning cold.

That night Alec put more wood on the fire he had been able to start to keep him warm. Then he crawled wearily into his shelter. Soon he was fast asleep.

03

He didn't know how long he had been sleeping when the Black's shrill scream awakened him. The top of the shed was on fire! Alec leaped to his feet and rushed outside. A strong wind was blowing, and instantly he saw what had happened. Sparks from his campfire had been blown upon the top of the shelter and had set fire to the dry wood.

Alec grabbed a turtle shell, filled it at the spring, and threw the water on the flames. He did this again and again, but the fire had too good a start and soon the whole shelter and two nearby trees were blazing.

The fire burned until early dawn, and when it was over Alec's shelter was gone. There was nothing for him to do but try to build a new one. The Black trotted ahead of him as he went toward the beach to look for some wood.

At the crest of the hill, Alec suddenly stopped. There below him was a ship anchored a few hundred yards off the island!

Then he heard voices, and saw a rowboat being drawn up on the beach by five men.

"You were right, Pat, there *is* someone on this island!" he heard one of the men shout. And the other said, "Sure, and I knew I saw the light of a big fire burning here last night!"

Alec shouted for joy. "We're going home, Black!" he
yelled to his horse. "We're going home!"

The sailors couldn't believe their eyes when they saw Alec, for he was a strange sight. His red hair was long and tangled, and his thin body, browned by the sun, was covered with only a few shreds of clothing. When Alec told the sailors how he had been pulled through the stormy sea by a big black horse, they thought he must be imagining things. But when he called the Black, and the fiery horse came running down the hill to him, the sailors could no longer doubt his word.

They stepped back in their fear of the Black, and watched with wonder in their eyes when Alec patted and coaxed the big black horse toward them. Then Alec said, "You'll take him, too, won't you? I can't leave him behind!"

"He's too wild. We couldn't take him. We couldn't handle him!" came the captain's answer.

"But *I* can handle him," Alec pleaded. The Black was still, his head turned toward the ship as if he understood what was going on. "Please," Alec said. "He saved my life. I can't leave him here alone. He'll die!"

"But how are you going to get him out there?" the captain asked, pointing to the anchored ship.

"He can swim," Alec answered eagerly. "He'll follow me. I know he will."

The captain talked to his men about it and then said, "Okay, son—you win. Now let's see you get him to the ship."

"Come on, Black," Alec said, standing up in the boat while the sailors began rowing slowly. "Come on, Black!" he urged, raising his voice. "Swim, Black! Swim!"

The big horse pawed the sand. He reared high in the air. He trusted Alec but not the strange men in the boat. He ran up and down the beach, snorting and neighing. Alec kept calling him to come as the boat moved farther and farther away from the beach.

Suddenly the Black plunged into the water and began swimming, following the boy he loved.

When they reached the big ship, the Black was swimming close to the rowboat. "Good boy," Alec whispered proudly to him.

The sailors went aboard, and soon they lowered a
long chain that was used in lifting heavy boxes onto
the ship. At the end of the chain hung a broad strap
that had to be put around the Black's stomach. How
was he going to do this, Alec wondered? He took the
strap in one hand and slid from the small boat into
the water. Then he called softly and the Black swam
toward him.

When Alec was alongside his horse he took a deep breath and sank below the surface. He swam under water, trying to get beneath the Black's stomach and come up on the other side of him. In that way he would get the strap around his horse. But one of the Black's hoofs struck him accidentally on the shoulder and he had to rise to the surface. He waited until the pain left his shoulder and then tried again. This time he swam deeper, and when he came up on the other side of the Black he buckled the strap tight around the horse. Then he called to the sailors to start the engine that would raise the chain.

Slowly the Black was lifted out of the water and high into the air. He thrashed his legs wildly in his fury. But at last he was safely on board the ship, and Alec was there to tell him that everything was all right.

The captain of the ship gave the Black a fine big stall, and Alec spent almost every hour with his horse. He gave him good things to eat, oats and bran and hay. Every day, too, he gave him an apple, for he'd found that the Black loved apples just as much as he did. And Alec told him that within a few days they would reach New York City, where his mother and father would meet the ship. The captain had sent them a message by radio, telling them that Alec was safe and on his way home. The message hadn't said, though, that he was bringing a horse home with him. Alec worried about this. What would his mother and father say when they saw the big horse? Would they let him keep him? He had already thought of a place to stable the Black. Down the street from where he lived on Long Island were an empty barn and a big field.

"That'll be your home," he told the Black, "and I'll take care of you."

When the ship reached New York City, Alec had his hands full getting the Black down the gangplank. It was evening, and the crowds and bright lights of the pier frightened the big horse. Several times he reared high on his hind legs, and his great body was hot and wet with fear.

Alec removed his sweater and tied it over the Black's eyes. He told him that *he* would be his eyes for a little while, and there was nothing to be afraid of. When the

Black's big body had stopped trembling, Alec knew it was safe to take him down the gangplank.

On the pier Alec's mother and father were waiting for him. They all put their arms around one another and stayed that way a long, long time. After that, they turned to the Black.

"He's mine," Alec told them.

They didn't say anything. They were afraid of the Black.

Alec told them not to be afraid, that the Black was the most wonderful horse in the whole wide world. And he told them how the Black had saved his life by pulling him through the terrible storm and onto the safe, sandy beach. "I wouldn't be here now, if it weren't for him. Please let me take him home. He's my horse forever and ever."

Tears were in his parents' eyes when Alec finished his long story. But even though they were very grateful to this big black horse for saving Alec's life, they were still terribly afraid of him. "He's so big, Alec," they said, "... so big and wild."

Alec turned to his horse. Yes, the Black was all they said, *so big and wild*. But how could he make them understand that if you loved him and were good to him, he would love you too and always be your friend?

Suddenly the Black's large nostrils opened wide as he sniffed the air about him. Then he walked forward. He went to Alec's mother and pushed his nose into her big coat pocket!

It happened so quickly that Alec's mother didn't have a chance to get away from him. Before she knew it, the big black horse had the apple from her pocket.

She had bought it from a man on the pier, thinking Alec would like to eat it on the way home.

Alec grinned and said, "He likes apples a lot, Mom, so now he's your friend too."

His mother and father put their hands on the Black's nose, patting him timidly. Alec watched them, knowing that everything had turned out all right and the Black was going *home*!

So the big black horse now lives in the old barn not far from Alec's house. Alec works hard, taking care of him and doing jobs after school so he can buy feed and apples for his horse. But he's very happy, and so is the Black. They're together and that's the way they had hoped it would be.